MARK DAVIS
CRAZY cars
for Crazy Kids

LITTLE HARE

Little Hare Books
4/21 Mary Street, Surry Hills
NSW 2010 AUSTRALIA

www.littleharebooks.com

First published in 2006

National Library of Australia
Cataloguing-in-Publication entry

David, Mark.

Crazy cars : for crazy kids.

For children.
ISBN 1 921049 19 7.

1. Automobiles - Juvenile fiction. I. Title.

A823.4

Designed by Wideopen.net.au
Produced by Phoenix Offset, Hong Kong
Printed in China

5 4 3 2 1

This book is called *Crazy Cars*, but it could just as easily have been called *Extremely Sensible Cars*. That's because it's full of sensible ideas.

I was on my way to a white-water rafting adventure not so long ago, when I got stuck for hours in a terrible traffic jam. Then, when I finally reached the river, it turned out that most of the adventure involved finding a parking space. There had to be a better way. For example, why couldn't I go white-water rafting *in* the car instead of waiting until I got there? And when I did get there, wouldn't it be great if my car could make its own parking space?

I rang several car companies and asked what they were doing to tackle these important issues, but they just made strange noises through the telephone and hung up on me. Clearly it was up to me to do something about it—to raise the standards of motoring. It was time to get practical with car design.

Rather than limit myself to white-water rafting alone, I started with a car that contained a whole luxury resort, but even that didn't solve all my problems. I still needed to take my dogs for a walk—why not invent another car for that? That was another worthwhile project, but I was still stuck looking for a place to park. It was only when I was well on the way to finishing the Park-o-matic that I realised it couldn't even make a decent piece of toast! So once again I found myself in the workshop…

It's been a long haul, but I believe that motoring is better for it. Driving has become the pleasure it always should have been. I'm satisfied that there are enough sensible ideas in this book to suit even the craziest kids. So strap on your seatbelts and enjoy the ride!

Luxury Resortster

Holidays are supposed to be fun—and the way I see it, the fun should start the moment your car leaves the garage.

Experience the thrills of white-water rafting without even leaving the road, or play a round of golf on the challenging 1-hole course. With a Luxury Resortster, you'll get to your holiday destination feeling like you've already had a holiday.

FEATURES

Customise your Resortster to suit your interests. Maybe you'd like to do some trout fishing at the traffic lights or perhaps some hang-gliding on the highway.

If you enjoy changing tyres, you'll love the Luxury Resortster!

Ground-hugging aerodynamics

DELUXE MODEL

Due to popular demand, the new deluxe model has all the features of the regular model but comes with brakes.

OPTIONAL EXTRAS

☆ Metallic paint, food hall, butler service

CHOOSE THE POT PLANT WHICH BEST MATCHES THE DESIRED STYLE OF RESORT

Rose bushes, for that touch of class

Palm trees, for the tropical look

...or Californian redwoods, for that forest retreat

Fido PoochCruiser

If dogs ruled the world, we'd all be driving cars like this one. Instead, the world is run by dog owners, who drive completely unsuitable cars. For the sake of our four-legged friends, I had to do something about it.

Your dogs will howl with delight when you drive home in a Fido PoochCruiser. Featuring all the latest developments in the science of dog recreation, the PoochCruiser allows precise fingertip control of feeding, exercise, rest and leisure for your canine companions.

FEATURES

☆ Never lose a dog, thanks to the transparent access tubes.

☆ The patented bone dispenser keeps them coming back for more.

☆ Set the treadmill to one of three dog-friendly speeds:

Tired Chihuahua

Reasonably fit Kelpie

Frantic Greyhound

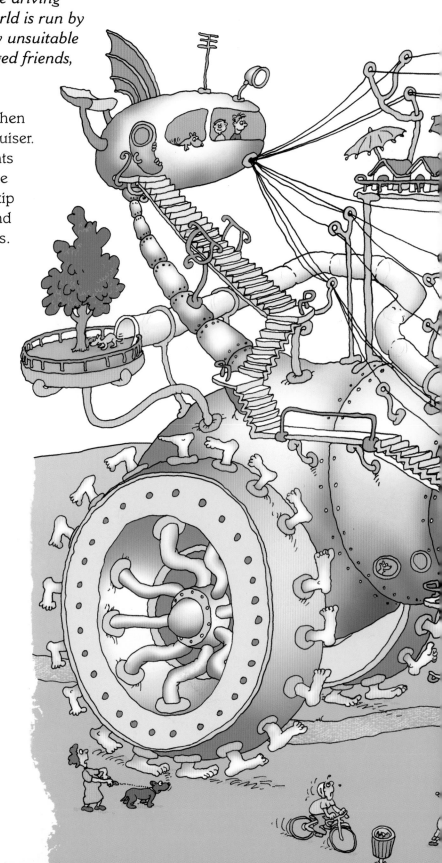

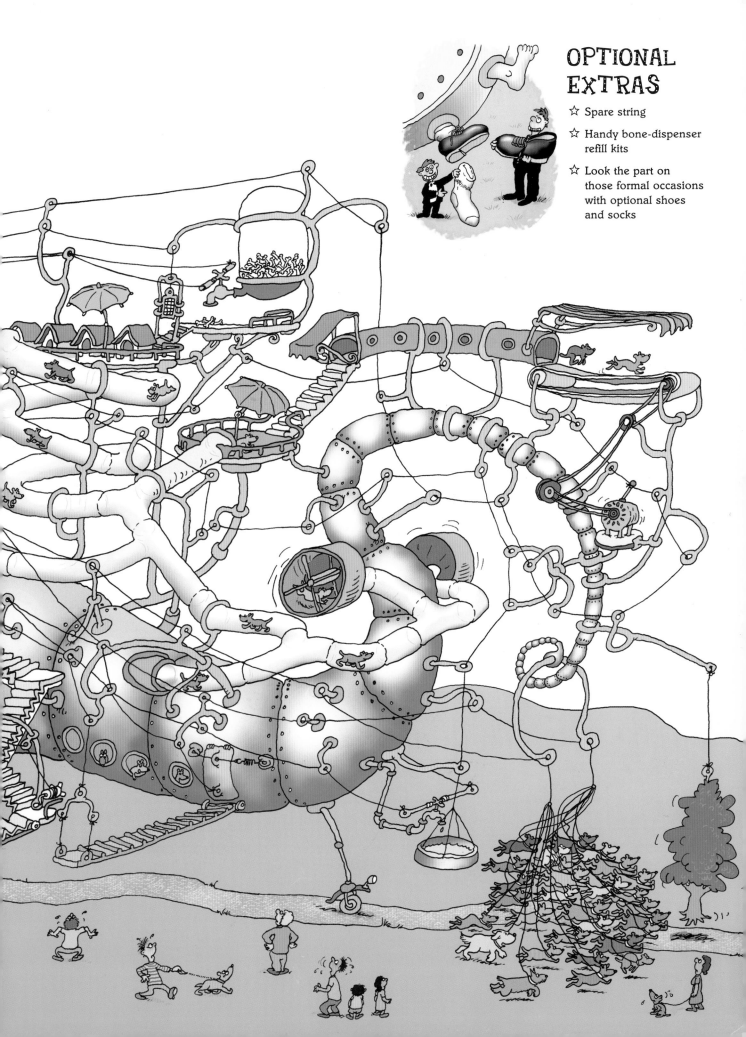

☆ Spare string

☆ Handy bone-dispenser refill kits

☆ Look the part on those formal occasions with optional shoes and socks

King Fisher

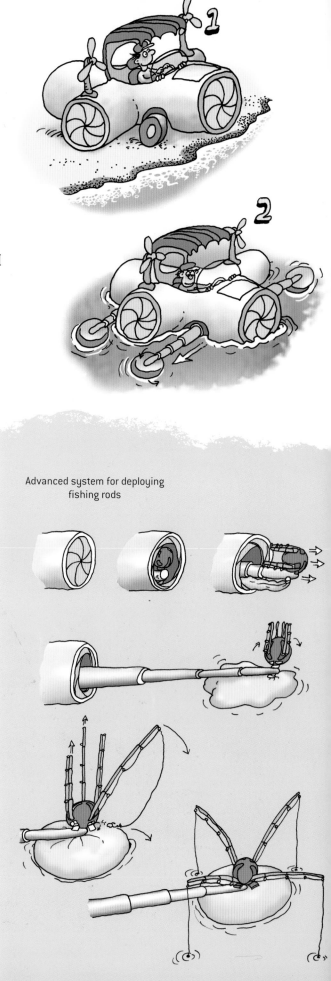

Everyone says we should eat less chips and more fish, but I couldn't find even one car that could catch fish properly! I decided to create my own…

You'll fill your boot with fish every time you go for a drive in the new King Fisher. Cruise the highway in comfortable style, then cruise the waterways to where the big ones are biting. Advanced fishing rod extension technology takes the hard work out of casting a line, leaving you free to think about how you're going to cook all those fish.

Before owning a
King Fisher

After owning a
King Fisher

Advanced system for deploying
fishing rods

FEATURES

Choose the bait that's right for your area. I employed a school of consultant salmon to design the bait packs, and made sure that only their favourites appear on the menu.

prawns   worms   artificial lures   slimy grey stuff

OPTIONAL EXTRAS

☆ Ice box

☆ Fish identification chart

☆ Waterproof joints, paint and panels

Park-o-matic

Recently I noticed it was getting harder and harder to find a good parking space. Here was a problem that needed a special kind of car—so I put together a team of parking specialists to come up with a solution.

This stylish vehicle comes with a range of revolutionary and fun ways to deal with all those cars—the ones that beat you to the best spaces. You'll always get the best park in a Park-o-matic!

FEATURES

☆ Driver-side air bag, in case of collisions.

☆ Get a clear view of the traffic, thanks to the high driver's seat position, which lets you see over the car in front—as well as see over trucks, trees and even buildings.

☆ With the advanced suspension you won't feel a bump when you hit the curb, or a tank, or a mountain.

Spiked wheels offer extra grip

(And something I'm still working on)

☆ Insurance cover for damage to other cars

Velocitree

My car was parked in the shade of a tree one day when I realised how much better it would be if I could take the shade with me. From this small idea, the Velocitree grew...

This car offers a mix of cool comfort and sporty performance rarely matched by other cars—or trees. Park where you want, as you'll never have to look for a shady spot again. Buy a whole forest of Velocitrees, and you and your friends can enjoy the wind in your leaves while you cruise the highways.

FEATURES

☆ Buy your car as a seedling or fully grown.

☆ Keep your Velocitree green with the easy-to-use watering system.

☆ Park your new Velocitree in the rain...

and watch it grow.

OPTIONAL EXTRAS

☆ Fertiliser

☆ Aphid spray

☆ Spare string

Chefrolet

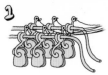

Bread lined up
ready for toasting

My mornings tend to be such a rush, I'm always running out of time for breakfast. The way I see it, if your car can take you places, then it should be able to do much, much more—like feed you.

The Chefrolet combines cruising with catering. It serves up porridge, toast, eggs and fruit, plus a cup of tea for the driver.

FEATURES

☆ Enjoy fresh milk in your porridge.

☆ The best milk comes from contented cows, and nothing keeps your cow contented like round-the-clock Cow Channel.

☆ Excellent economy
    Fuel consumption: 10 litres per 100 kilometres
    Milk delivery: One glass of milk to the kilometre

COOKING THE EGGS

Suction cup picks
up an egg

Egg swings onto a
sharp spike

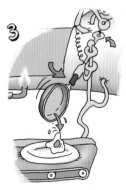

The frying pan swings around
to serve your cooked egg
sunny side up

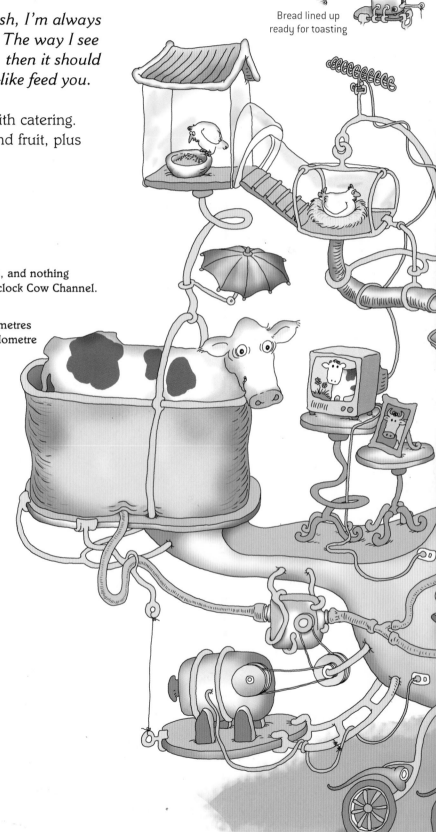

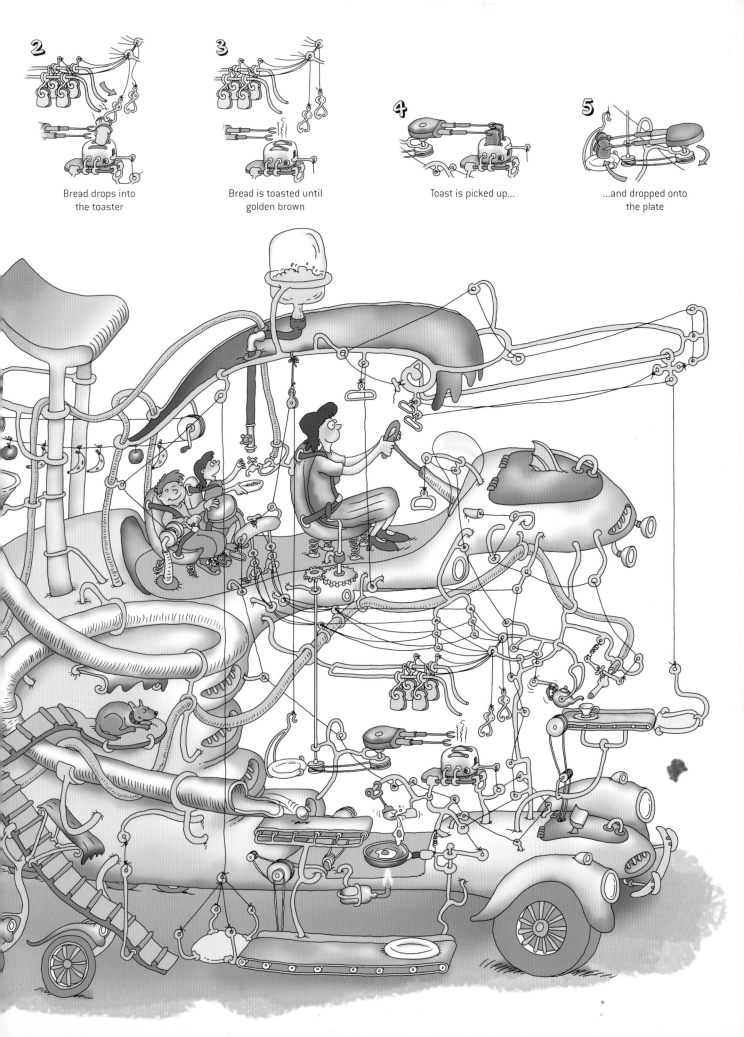

2 Bread drops into the toaster

3 Bread is toasted until golden brown

4 Toast is picked up...

5 ...and dropped onto the plate

Millispeed

I'm a big fan of bugs. They have all sorts of ways of getting around. Once I based a car on a moth, but I ended up with a car that kept driving into lights. So I tried a millipede instead and got this much more practical model.

A Millispeed lets you reach all the places a millipede can, but faster—and unlike the millipede, this car is also at home on the highway.

FEATURES

☆ It will seem like you're getting places in no time. In fact, the front of the car will be at the shops before the back has even left the garage!

☆ Millispeed not long enough? Add more bits to the middle.

OPTIONAL EXTRAS

☆ Roof racks

☆ Add some handy storage with the tow bar and trailer

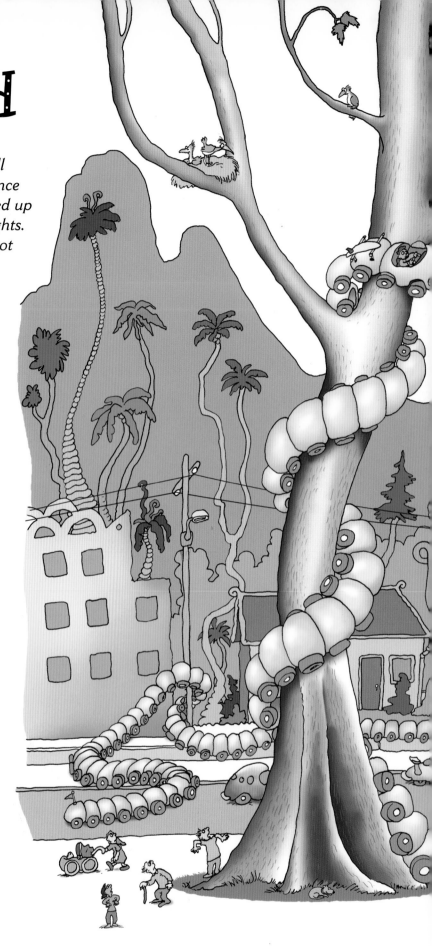

Crazytrailer

After designing a lot of very sensible cars, I still felt that something was missing. I needed a trailer, except it had to be better than a normal trailer. I needed the Crazytrailer.

Do you hate having to leave all your best stuff behind when you go out for a drive? You can take it all with you in a Crazytrailer. Your swimming pool, grandfather, boat and dog—there's a Crazytrailer solution for everything.

OPTIONAL EXTRA

☆ Get even more storage with the new multi-storey model

Windster

One especially windy day, while I was watching the cars blow past my top-floor window, I had an idea. I realised right then that the world needed a good windy-day type of car. That's what led to the Windster.

While other cars try to cut down their wind resistance, this one thrives on it. In fact, the more blustery the better! Turn a wintry gale into a blast down the highway in your Windster.

FEATURES

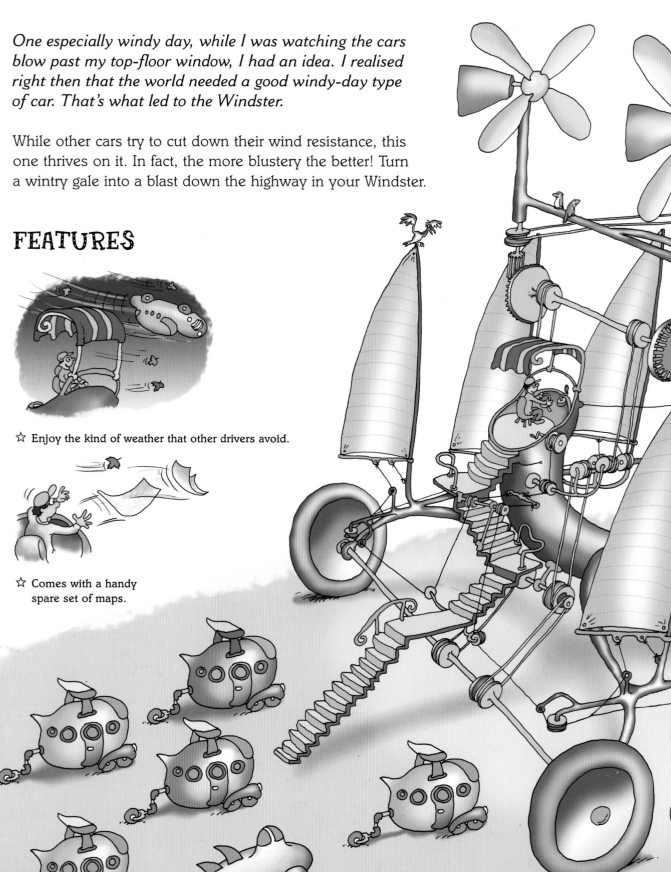

☆ Enjoy the kind of weather that other drivers avoid.

☆ Comes with a handy spare set of maps.

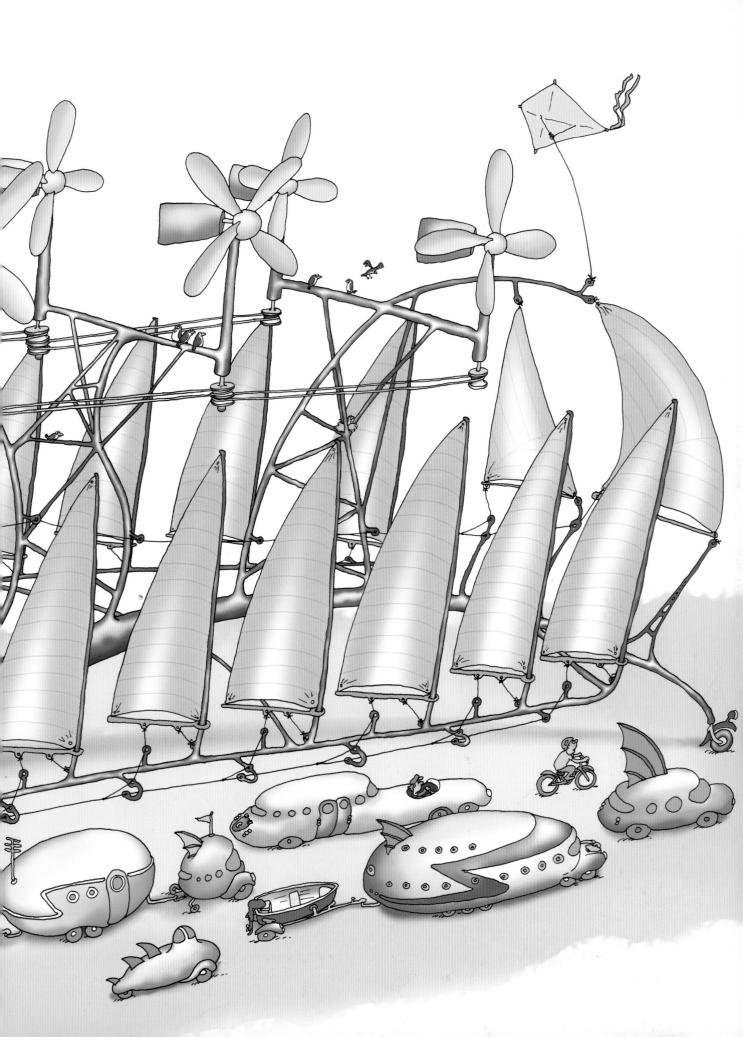

Spiderwagon

Now don't get me wrong—I've got nothing against wheels. But wheels have their limits, and who wants a car with limits?

Is peak-hour traffic slowing down to a crawl? Then it's time you climbed into a Spiderwagon, the car that crawls like no other. With road-hugging 8-leg drive, you'll love its performance and admire its off-road handling even more.

FEATURES

☆ No need for a garage.

☆ Always find a parking space.

☆ Wrap up your own shopping.

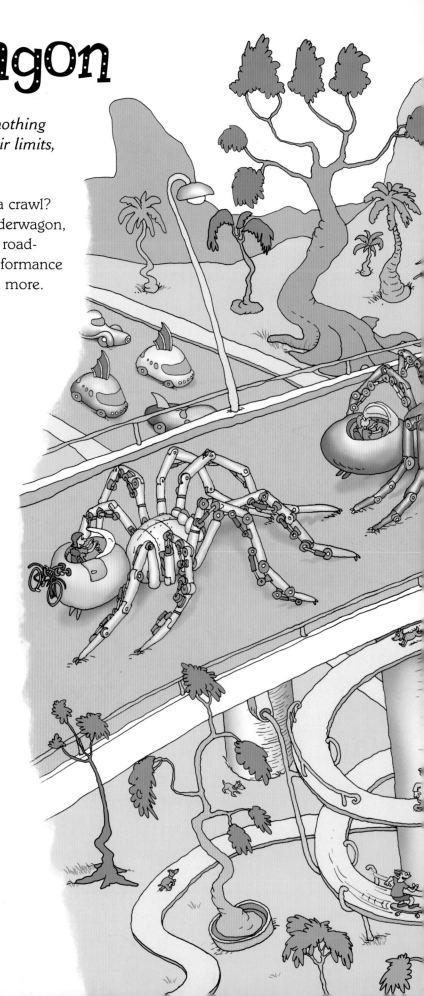

Speedrunner

I spent years trying to run faster than dogs, but finally had to admit I didn't have the legs for it. I needed help in the form of a special kind of car. I needed a Speedrunner.

The Speedrunner lets you keep up with your fastest dog, turning that speedy pooch into a valuable power source. It's all made possible using the latest in air-flow design, ensuring your Speedrunner—and dog—don't become airborne, even while cornering.

FEATURES

☆ Change your power source quickly and easily.

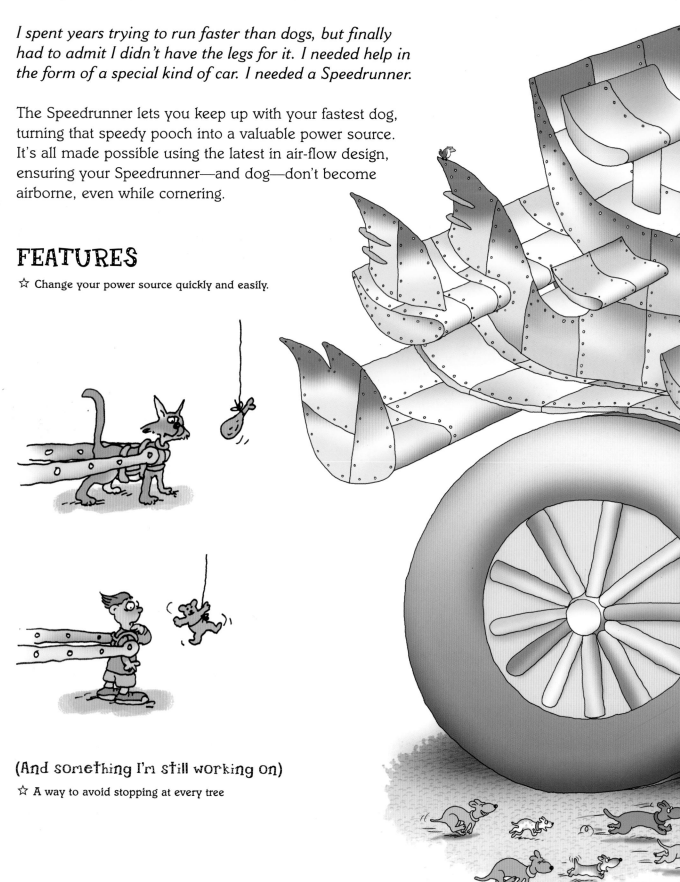

(And something I'm still working on)

☆ A way to avoid stopping at every tree

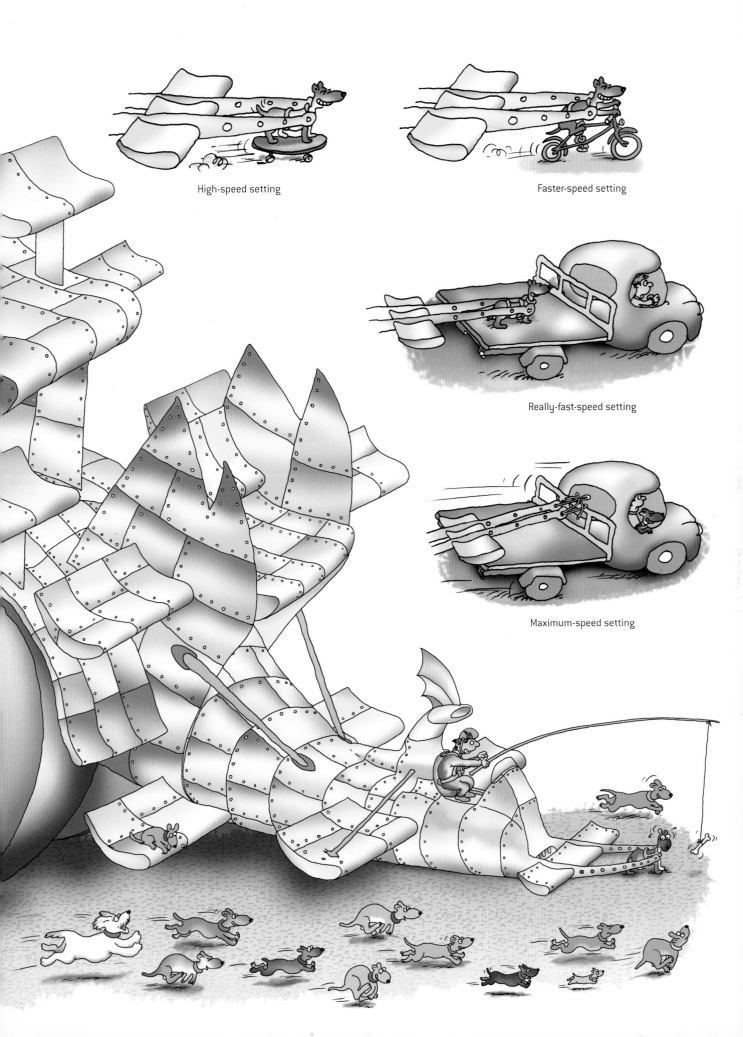

High-speed setting

Faster-speed setting

Really-fast-speed setting

Maximum-speed setting

RollerRoadster

The only problem with rollercoasters, it seems to me, is after all that riding you still end up right where you started. I couldn't ignore this problem any longer, so I invented the RollerRoadster.

Are you stuck in a traffic jam and looking for a thrill? Then it's time for a new type of car. The RollerRoadster turns a boring trip to the shops into a hair-raising ride of twists, loops and gut-wrenching turns. Your friends will be so keen to get a lift home you'll be able to sell tickets! You'll wonder why all cars don't come fitted with a rollercoaster.

FEATURES

☆ Enjoy your ride even while stopped at traffic lights.

☆ Every RollerRoadster has a comfortable rest room specially designed for people who don't cope very well with rides.

OPTIONAL EXTRAS

☆ Ticket booth

☆ Ghost train conversion kit

☆ Dining car

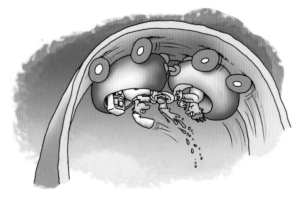

Optional dining car

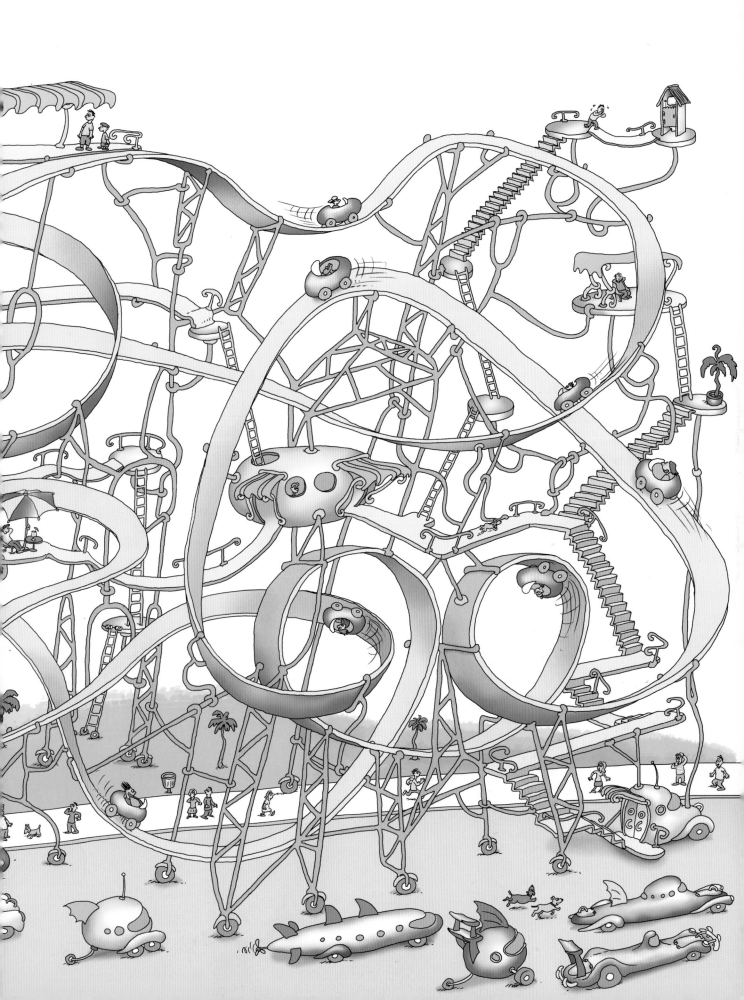

Supercommuter

I can't see why someone should commute to the office if they can commute in the office. So I bolted some wheels onto a regular building and followed it from there. In fact, I'm still following it, and at the speed it's been going lately, it looks like I'll never catch it!

Designed by the architects of city office blocks, the Supercommuter brings new meaning to the term 'mobile office'. Look out for one on a road near you.

FEATURES

☆ All floors have much better views than regular cars.

☆ Real estate agents say that location is important. Now you can move to a better location without having to clean out your desk.

☆ Choose your model based on the size of your business.

Small business model

Big business model

Taskbuggy

I always seem to have more things to do than I can squeeze into a normal day. So I decided to find a way to get some of those things done while I was on the road.

Why not meet a friend at a cafe while you're driving to the movies, then get your hair cut on the trip home? How about taking a walk to the shops while you're driving to the beach? You can do it all in a Taskbuggy!

FEATURES

☆ Customise your Taskbuggy for the chores you need done. For example:

Grab a bread roll at the bakery

Pick up some cash at an automatic teller machine

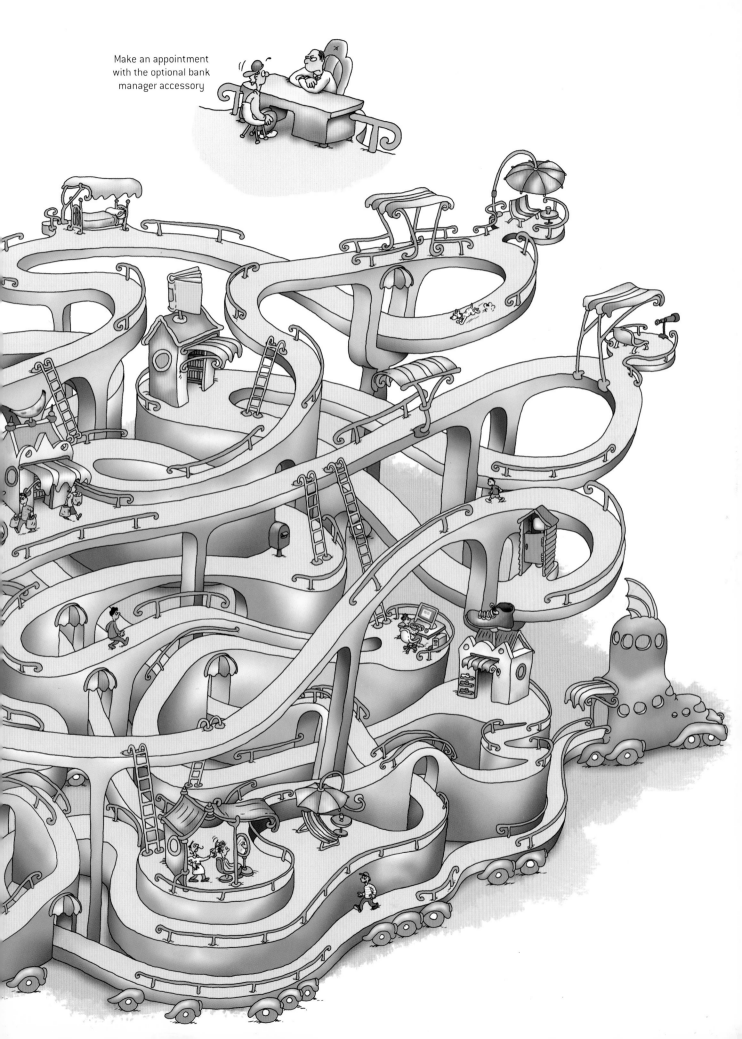

Make an appointment with the optional bank manager accessory

Decibel Clangster

No serious car collection would be complete without this one!

Don't you hate it when someone pulls up beside you, and their radio is louder than yours? Those days are over with the Decibel Clangster— the greatest advance in motoring since the air horn.

Let the whole neighbourhood know you're coming with the kind of music only this car can make!

FEATURES

☆ Dual exhaust pipes make sure you hit the right note.

☆ Even better than a full orchestra. While an orchestra has only four sections (strings, woodwind, brass and percussion), the Clangster has all those plus a noisy engine.

OPTIONAL EXTRA

☆ Karaoke model